THIS BLOOMSBURY BOOK
BELONGS TO

Rosemary

from Sadie Christmas 2005

For Rachel, very dearly missed – *SR*
For Will, with love – *JJ*

First published in Great Britain in 2002 by Bloomsbury Publishing Plc
38 Soho Square, London, W1D 3HB
This paperback edition first published in 2003

Text copyright © Shen Roddie 2002
Illustrations copyright © Jenny Jones 2002
The moral right of the author and illustrator has been asserted

A CIP catalogue record of this book is available from the British Library
ISBN 0 7475 6115 X

Printed in Hong Kong by South China Printing Co. Ltd
10 9 8 7 6 5 4 3

SANDBEAR

SHEN RODDIE AND JENNY JONES

BLOOMSBURY
CHILDREN'S
BOOKS

Out in the dunes, a wild wind blew and
the sands shivered. It made quivery sand
waves and puffy little sandhills.
"I can see a sandbear in here!" said Hare,
looking at a funny little mound. Hare dug
some sand and flung it at the sandhill.
He sloshed some water from his bucket
to wet it.

"There!" he said as he patted a body.
"You're very podgy. You'll make a
jolly sandbear!"

"A body's no good without a head," thought Hare. So he tossed some sand over Sandbear's body.

"A funny-looking head but what great ears! You won't mind, will you, Bear?" laughed Hare.

"As for your eyes, these bitsy pebbles will do," said Hare as he popped them on Sandbear's face.

"They're all I can find in a hurry!"

"A bear needs a sniffer!" said Hare, plonking a nose-sized piece of driftwood where a bear's nose should be.

"It's not a bear's nose I know, but you'll get used to it!"

"Just as you'll get used to this!" said Hare as he jabbed a finger under bear's nose.

"A pinhole mouth!" laughed Hare.

Then Hare traced out two short legs.
"That'll do for a bear who's not going
anywhere!" he said.

Hare stood back to take a look.
"I say! You look just like a friend!"
he cried excitedly. "We could picnic together,
you and I. But you'll need hands for that."

Hare grabbed a handful of sand.
Then he let go of it.
"Oh bother!" he groaned. "It takes
for ever to make a pair of hands!
I need something quick and easy!"

"I know!" said Hare, shoving a blade of grass into Sandbear's side. "A friendly one-armed bandit!" chuckled Hare.

"I'd love to make you handsomer but it's hard work and I haven't all day. I've got to go! It's munchtime! See you tomorrow if the wild winds don't blow."

"Bye, Sandbear!" Hare called as he hopped away.

Not long after, the wild winds blew.
"Brrrr ... I'm cold," said Sandbear,
brushing sand from his eye. "I wish
I had a coat to keep warm."

"I know! I'll gallop quickly to the woods.
Clop! Clop! The woods would keep me
warm," thought Sandbear happily.

But Sandbear could not gallop quickly.
His legs were too short. So he shuffled
slowly to the woods where a cold bear
could be warm.

Sandbear shuffled a long, long way.

He stumbled across a sandcrab.

He stepped on a grass frog.

"That's my tail you're treading on, Sandbear!" said a field mouse. "Oops! Sorry!"

"If only I had big, bright eyes!" thought Sandbear.

"I'm hungry and every hungry bear
loves a farm," he said.
He found a carrot but could not pull
it out. His grass hand was no good!
So he dug at it with his nose and
out it popped!
"Yum!" thought Sandbear.
He tried to eat it. But his mouth
was far too small!
"Silly Hare!" thought Sandbear.

Just then, he heard a cry.
"Help! Somebody help!"
"It's coming from over *there*,"
said Sandbear.

Sandbear shuffled as fast as he could.
"Where are you?" he called.
"Here!" wailed a voice.

"It seems to be coming from here!" thought Sandbear. Sandbear looked down a deep, dark hole.

"I see two floppy ears!" he cried. "It's Hare!"

Hare had fallen into a deep pit. He was shaking with fright.

"Whistle a happy tune, Hare, while I get you out!" said Sandbear.

"How?" asked Hare.

"By doing my very best!" said Sandbear. Sandbear looked round for a rope but there wasn't one.

He leant over.

"Here! Hold on to my hand and don't let go," said Sandbear as he lowered his grass hand as far down as he could.

"Have you got it, friend?" asked Sandbear.

"Yes!" replied Hare and as soon as he said that, Sandbear lost his hand! Hare had pulled it off!

"Oh dear!" cried Hare.
"Oh dear!" sighed Sandbear.

Then without a further thought, Sandbear
said: "I'm coming!" and he slid down,
down, down the deep, dark hole.
"Hare!" cried Sandbear as he disappeared
into the darkness. "Hop out quick!"
Hare leapt on top of Sandbear and
jumped out.
"Thanks, Sandbear! You've saved my life!"
said Hare, peering into the pit.

But all Hare saw was a pile of sand with
two bitsy pebbles, a piece of driftwood
and a blade of grass.

There was no Sandbear.
Sandbear was no more!

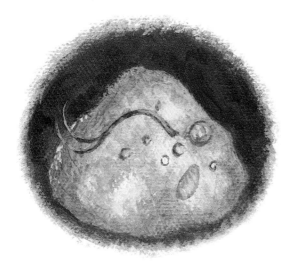

"Sandbear! Oh Sandbear!" cried Hare,
a big tear bursting down his cheek.
"You're in there! I know you are!"
cried Hare.
"I'll get you out! You'll see!"
Hurriedly, Hare grabbed a spade.
Then carefully, very carefully, Hare
dug Sandbear out.
He piled him high.
Carefully, very carefully, he drizzled
water to wet him.
Hare patted a shape.
A jolly, podgy shape.
A shape with two strong legs.

Then he made a head.
A familiar, peculiar Sandbear head.

Hare shaped two arms for Sandbear's bearhugs.

Then he hunted for a pair of shiny, black pebbles.
"There, bright eyes!" said Hare.

Hare put Sandbear's nose back on.
"So I will always know it's you!"
said Hare.

And to stop Sandbear from freezing when the wild winds blew, Hare lent him his hat and waistcoat.

"I haven't forgotten your mouth, Sandbear! How would you like it, my dear friend?" asked Hare.

Sandbear s - t - r - e - t - c - h - e d out his arms. "I thought so!" said Hare.

"BIG! Perfect for a bear dinner!"

At the word 'dinner', Sandbear picked Hare
up with his big bear arms. He swung him
high in the air. Then dropped him – plop! –
on to his big bear shoulders.
"Come on, my friend! Off to the woods
we go. It's picnic time! Remember?"
said Sandbear happily.

And with the wild wind behind them,
they vanished into the woods ahead.

Acclaim for Sandbear ...

'This ingenious picture book tale tells a warm story about friendship'
Copley News Service

Enjoy more great picture books from Bloomsbury ...

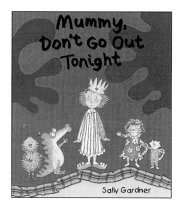

Mummy, Don't Go Out Tonight
Sally Gardner

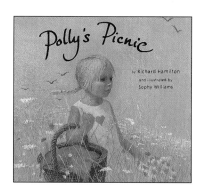

Polly's Picnic
Richard Hamilton & Sophy Williams

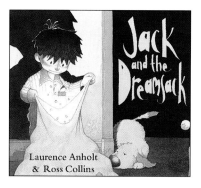

Jack and the Dreamsack
Laurence Anholt & Ross Collins

Please Don't Chat to the Bus Driver
Shen Roddie & Jill Newton

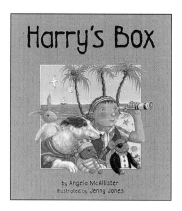

Harry's Box
Angela McAllister & Jenny Jones